DISCARDED FROM
GARFIELD COUNTY

GARFIELD COUNTY LIBRARIES
Carbondale Branch Library
320 Sopris Ave
Carbondale, CO 81623
(970) 963-2889 – Fax (970) 963-8573
www.gcpld.org

Courtesy of Zelma Redding

OTIS REDDING (1941–1967) was a singer, songwriter, and producer often referred to as the King of Soul™. Known for releasing such acclaimed songs as "These Arms of Mine," "Try a Little Tenderness™," "Hard to Handle," and "(Sittin' on) The Dock of the Bay," Redding is considered to be one of the most influential singers and songwriters of all time. He received two GRAMMYs as well as a GRAMMY Lifetime Achievement Award, and was inducted into the Rock & Roll Hall of Fame and the Songwriters Hall of Fame. To learn more, visit: otisredding.com.

RACHEL MOSS (illustrator) was born in Jamaica and studied animation in England at the University for the Creative Arts. She now lives in Jamaica where she spends her days illustrating children's books such as *African* with song lyrics by Peter Tosh, *I Am a Promise* by Shelly Ann Fraser Pryce, *Abigail's Glorious Hair*, and *Milo & Myra Learn Manners with Mr. Mongoose*.

❧ ❧ ❧

No part of this book may be reproduced, stored in a retrieval system, or transmitted in any form, by any means, including mechanical, electronic, photocopying, recording, or otherwise, without the prior written consent of the publisher.

"Respect"
Written by Otis Redding
Courtesy of Irving Music, Inc.
Used by Permission. All Rights Reserved.

LyricPop is a children's picture book collection by LyricVerse and Akashic Books.

lyricverse

Published by Akashic Books
Song lyrics ©1965 Otis Redding
Illustrations ©2020 Rachel Moss

ISBN: 978-1-61775-844-7
Library of Congress Control Number: 2020937302
First printing

Printed in China

Akashic Books
Brooklyn, New York
Twitter: @AkashicBooks
Facebook: AkashicBooks
E-mail: info@akashicbooks.com
Website: www.akashicbooks.com

Respect

song lyrics by
OTIS REDDING

illustrations by
RACHEL MOSS

Ooh, your kisses

sweeter than honey

And guess what?

So is my money

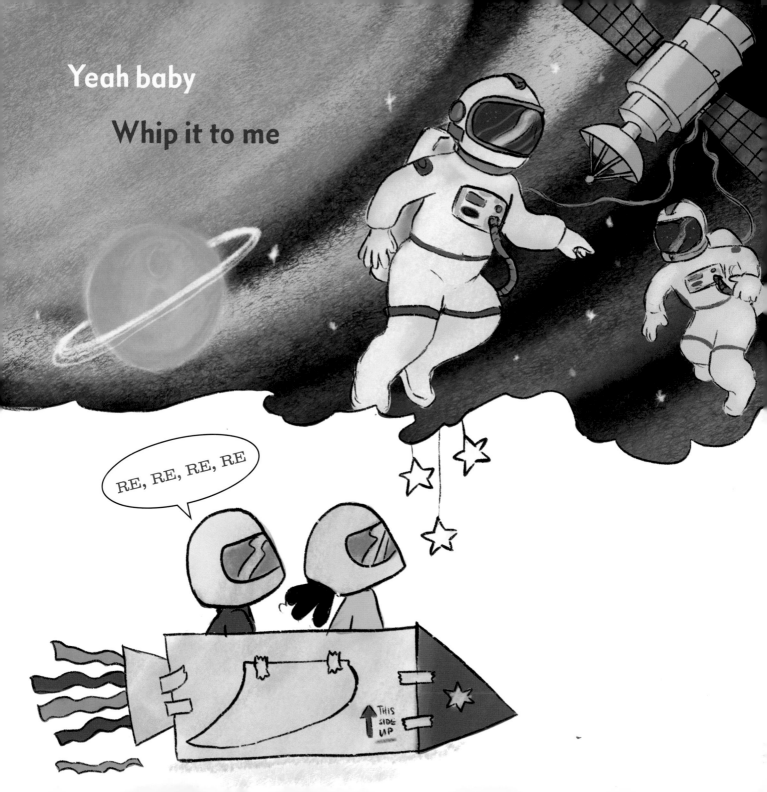

When you get home, now

Find out what it means to me

Take care,
TCB

Oh

SOCK IT TO ME

SOCK IT TO ME

SOCK IT TO ME

SOCK IT TO ME

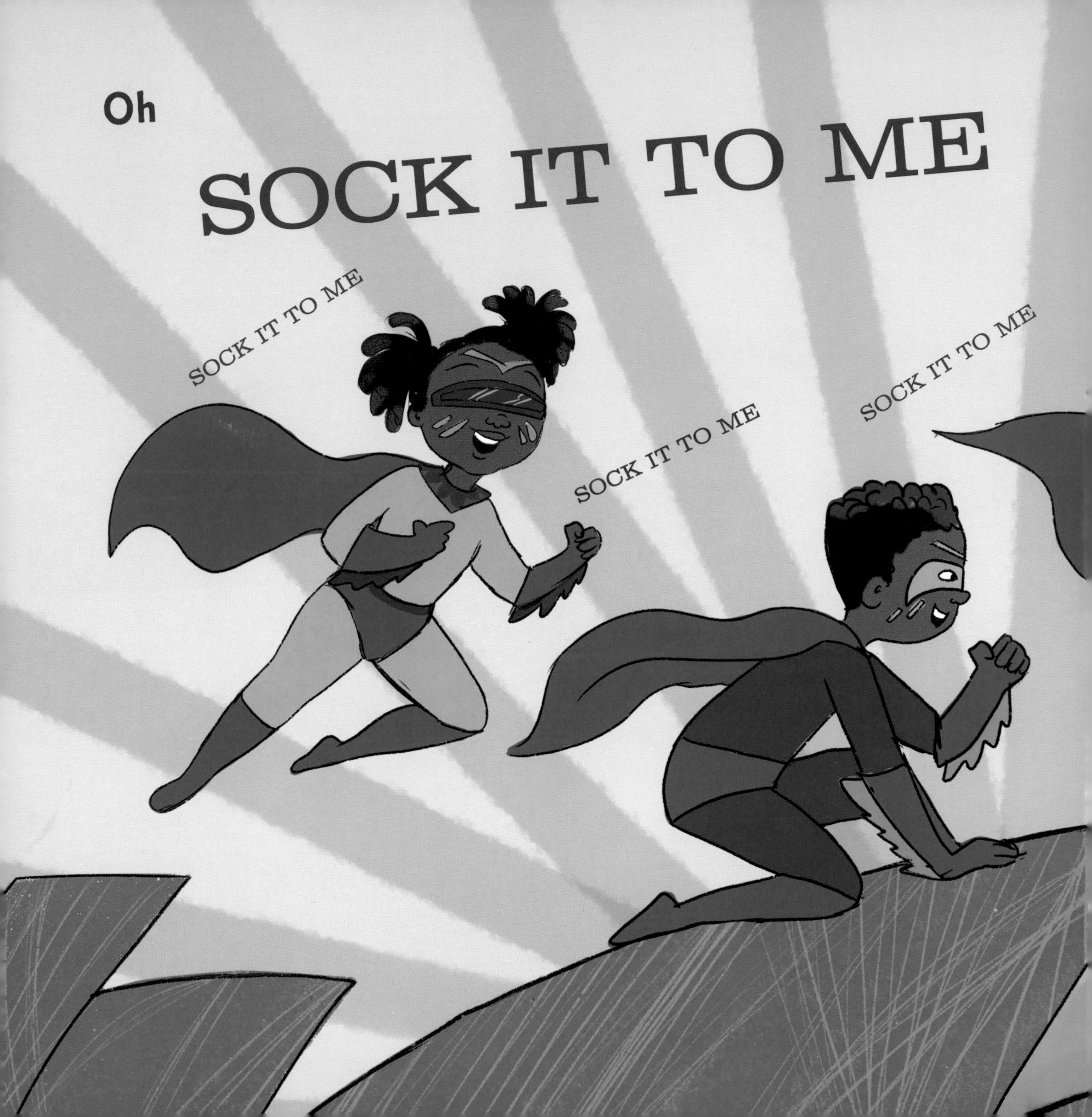

When you come home

Or you might walk in   and find that I'm

gone

LOOK OUT FOR THESE LyricPop TITLES

African SONG LYRICS BY PETER TOSH
ILLUSTRATIONS BY RACHEL MOSS

(Sittin' on) The Dock of the Bay
SONG LYRICS BY OTIS REDDING AND STEVE CROPPER
ILLUSTRATIONS BY KAITLYN SHEA O'CONNOR

Don't Stop SONG LYRICS BY CHRISTINE MCVIE
ILLUSTRATIONS BY NUSHA ASHJAEE

Good Vibrations
SONG LYRICS BY MIKE LOVE AND BRIAN WILSON
ILLUSTRATIONS BY PAUL HOPPE

Humble and Kind SONG LYRICS BY LORI MCKENNA
ILLUSTRATIONS BY KATHERINE BLACKMORE

Move the Crowd
SONG LYRICS BY ERIC BARRIER AND WILLIAM GRIFFIN
ILLUSTRATIONS BY KIRK PARRISH

These Boots Are Made for Walkin'
SONG LYRICS BY LEE HAZLEWOOD, ILLUSTRATIONS BY RACHEL MOSS

We Got the Beat SONG LYRICS BY CHARLOTTE CAFFEY
ILLUSTRATIONS BY KAITLYN SHEA O'CONNOR

We're Not Gonna Take It SONG LYRICS BY DEE SNIDER
ILLUSTRATIONS BY MARGARET MCCARTNEY

GARFIELD COUNTY
LIBRARIES
9677

What Does "Respect" Mean to You?

Otis Redding's song "Respect" has been enjoyed for generations, and is a celebration of the concept of respect, but what does respect really mean? In some ways, it is a measure of how you feel about yourself or others. In other ways, it is a measure of how you *treat* yourself and others. In every way, it's important to try to understand what other people experience in order to share respect with them. Let's explore what respect means to you!

1. How do you feel when you respect yourself? Does it make you feel happy? Proud? Frustrated? Tired?

2. How does respecting others make you feel?

3. Can you give an example of something you did that showed someone you respected him or her?

4. Can you give an example of something someone else did that made you respect him or her?

5. Can you give an example of something someone else did that showed a *lack* of respect to you or to others?

6. Can you respect someone even if you are mad at him or her?